EGYPTIAN TALES

THE PLOT ON THE PYRAMID

Bloomsbury Education
An imprint of Bloomsbury Publishing Plc

50 Bedford Square
London
WC1B 3DP
UK

1385 Broadway
New York
NY 10018
USA

www.bloomsbury.com

BLOOMSBURY and the Diana logo are trademarks of Bloomsbury Publishing Plc

First published in Great Britain 2004
This paperback edition published in 2017

A catalogue record for this book is available from the British Library.

ISBN

PB: 978 1 4729 4215 9
epub: 978 1 4729 5250 9
epdf: 978 1 4729 5249 3

2 4 6 8 10 9 7 5 3 1

Typeset by Newgen Knowledge Works (P) Ltd., Chennai, India

Printed and bound in UK by CPI Group (UK) ltd, Croydon CR0 4YY

TERRY DEARY

EGYPTIAN TALES

THE PLOT ON THE PYRAMID

Illustrated by Helen Flook

BLOOMSBURY EDUCATION
AN IMPRINT OF BLOOMSBURY

LONDON OXFORD NEW YORK NEW DELHI SYDNEY

CHAPTER 1
River and Rat

Nephoris sat by the edge of the mud-brown river and threw a stone into it. She was a tall girl and made her little brother Pere look tiny.

A light wind kept her cool and the rustling reeds seemed the only sound in the world. "Perfect," she said.

Of course that was before her mother called her home.

"River," Pere said. He picked up a stone and tried to copy Nephoris's throwing. But he forgot to let go and threw himself into the dirty water.

Nephoris shook her head, paddled into the cool water and pulled him out.

"It's Akhet," she told him.

The little boy's round face crinkled into a frown. "No Akhet. River."

She sat beside him and watched the graceful ibis birds land and stalk through the shallows, looking for food.

"I mean it's the time of the year – Akhet. The time when the river rises. It floods our fields and makes the corn grow. Akhet brings us food."

"Food," Pere repeated. Pere liked food.

Nephoris smiled. There weren't many restful days like this. Days when she could sit in the sun and play with Pere.

She had
to weed
the fields...

... fetch water...

... grind corn
or bake bread.

She'd done it ever since she was as young as Pere. But not at Akhet.

"When Akhet comes we can't work in the fields. So we get days like today. Peaceful days," she sighed.

Of course that was before her mother called her home. In the years to come Nephoris would never think of Akhet as the peaceful time again.

Pere took a fistful of mud and made it into a little pile. "Pyramid," he said.

Nephoris nodded. "Yes, Daddy is working on the pyramid for the King. Most of the men of Lisht are helping to build it because they can't work in the fields at Akhet. Poor Dad. We have idle days and he works harder than ever."

Pere made his chubby hand into a fist and smashed it down on top of his mud pile. "Pyramid!" he giggled.

"Poor pyramid," Nephoris said. "King Amenemhat is our god, you know. He makes the river flood the fields and makes the corn grow. That's why we are building Amenemhat a huge pyramid. Build Amenemhat another pyramid," she said.

As Pere piled up the mud, a ripple from the river washed it away. The river was rising quickly now. Amenemhat was doing his magic.

Pere frowned at the river and his ruined pyramid. "Naughty!" he said and slapped the water. It splashed up and soaked his angry face. Nephoris laughed. Life was good.

Then her mother called her home.

Her shrill voice carried over the quiet fields. "Neph-or-iiis!"

Neph-or-iiis!

"Mama!" Pere said and struggled to his feet. He had sharp ears and heard her first. Nephoris quickly washed his muddy legs and hands, scooped him up and ran along the dusty path towards their small mud house.

Meanwhile...

At the Pyramid of Lisht their father, Yenini, was getting more and more angry...

CHAPTER 2
Peril at the Pyramid

Yenini's face was red. Red with the heat of the midday sun. Red with the strain of pulling a pyramid block almost to the top of Amenemhat's pyramid. But, most of all, red with rage. Rage at the fat little bully, Antef.

Thirty men from Lisht made up a team of workers – the Boat Gang, they called themselves. They were proud of being the best of the hundred gangs that worked on the pyramid.

But the pharaoh had put Antef in charge – Antef with his perfumed wig and beard-wig, pot belly and wicked tongue.

The Boat Gang were free men. They worked for the love of King Amenemhat. Antef treated them like slaves – like the prisoners of war who were forced to work and beaten.

The day had started badly. Their massive stone, big as a house, had slipped off the barge that carried it over the Nile. They had to fasten ropes around it and drag it through the mud and onto the shore.

Yenini was a little worried that they would not get it up the pyramid before sunset. He didn't like the Boat Gang to fail. They never had before.

Then they heaved it onto a wooden sledge and the sledge cracked. It was an old one and Antef should have got them a better one.

Yenini was a bit upset by that.

The cracked sledge was harder to pull and it took them most of the morning to get it to the foot of the pyramid. Yenini was getting hungry. He had a lunch bag at his belt. When the sun passed the peak of the pyramid they could take a rest and eat at the shadowed side of the tomb.

But the sledge stuck on the ramp that led to the top.

Yenini was annoyed.

"Come on, Boat Gang," he cried. "Put your backs into it. There's a neat little hole at the top just waiting for this stone. And there's an even bigger hole in my stomach waiting for my dinner!"

The men laughed and tried harder. They sweated and strained and the huge stone moved upwards.

That was when Antef really upset them. He walked behind them and watched them.

"Laughing are you? Laughing. You are the biggest bunch of brainless beetles on this pyramid and all you can do is laugh. You can't move one little stone and you think it's funny?" he jeered and cracked his leather whip. It snapped in the air close to Yenini's nose.

"Hang on, Antef," Yenini said. "It's your fault that we have this cracked old sledge. It's your job to see we get the best." He was getting angry.

The stone reached the edge of the hole and the Boat Gang began to turn it so it would slide down neatly into the space.

Antef shook his whip in Yenini's face. "I am the servant of Amenemhat. It is the king who tells me what my job is. It's not your job to tell me my job. It's my job to tell you your job," he gabbled. "That's my job and I'm doing my job – so you do your job or my job will be to send you to the king to be punished."

"Don't threaten me," Yenini roared. He let go of the rope and stepped towards Antef. The little man jumped back in fear. His foot slipped on the edge of the hole and he slipped back into it.

The hole was just too deep for him to climb out. "Throw me a rope you desert snakes, you river rats, you savage scorpions, you... you... slimy ox dung!"

Yenini was red with rage. "It is time for lunch."

"You take lunch when I say you can take lunch! The king is coming this afternoon. He wants to see this stone in place. You will *not* stop for lunch. I forbid it," Antef wailed. "Get me out of here!"

The Boat Gang looked at each other. They dropped the ropes and walked back down the pyramid for a rest.

Meanwhile...

Back in the village Nephoris was carrying Pere home...

CHAPTER 3
The Slipping Stone

Yenini's family lived in a village on the edge of Lisht. That morning the people were working in the shade of the houses but one man worked in the full glare of the sun.

Using precious cedar wood, the artist Oneney was building a large statue.

"Big man," Pere said.

"Statue," Nephoris explained. "It's a statue of King Amenemhat. When he dies the statue will go inside the pyramid with the king's mummy."

The king's statue was almost finished. It was dressed in a white kilt and carrying a shepherd's crook. The life-sized model had one leg raised as if it was striding forward.

Beside it stood a finished model. A small round man in a wig, beard wig and purple robes, no taller than Nephoris.

"That's a model of Antef, the work-driver," Nephoris told her brother. "That will go in the pyramid too, so the dead king has company. Dad doesn't like Antef."

"Naughty man," Pere said and slapped the model.

Oneney was painting the crown on Amenemhat's head a bright red. A bowl was full of red paint.

"Blood," Pere said as Nephoris carried him past the artist.

Oneney shook his head. "No, young Pere. Beetles. I crush beetles to make the red colour."

Nephoris shuddered but Pere just looked puzzled.

"Your mother is looking for you," Oneney told her.

"I heard her calling. What does she want?" Nephoris asked.

Oneney shrugged.

Nephoris's mother stood at the door of their house holding a small package wrapped in cloth.

"What's wrong?" Nephoris asked.

Her mother held out the parcel. "Last night the cat caught a rat and left it in the middle of the floor – a nice present for us. I didn't want Pere picking it up and chewing at it. You know what he's like..."

"Rat," Pere said and licked his lips.

"This morning your father set off for the pyramid to work and I packed him some bread and onion like I always do," her mother went on.

"Yes," Nephoris said.

"Well... when I went to throw the rat away I opened the parcel and found the bread and onion!" she moaned.

"So," Nephoris grinned, "when Dad opens his lunch parcel he'll find..."

"Rat!" Pere said.

"Exactly! He'll be furious! He's in a bad temper all the time these days. That Antef bullies the workers all day

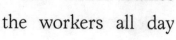

long from sunrise to sunset. Your dad comes home and he's full of fury. If he goes without food all day he will be as horrible as... as... "

"Rat," Pere said.

"Exactly," Mother agreed. "A big, bad-tempered rat." She looked up at the clear sky. The sun was not far from its highest point. "They'll be stopping soon for a break," she said. "You have to get this food to him before they stop!"

"Don't worry, Mum," Nephoris said. "I can run faster than anyone in this village. Give me the food."

She put her brother on the ground, took

the parcel and sped towards the site of
the pyramid.

The sun ran on. Nephoris ran on. Her
black hair flowed behind her and her long
legs raised clouds of dust. "I'm winning,
Sun, I'm winning," she cried.

At last she reached the wall around the
site and ran up to the first gang leader
she could find. "Boat Gang," she panted.
"Where will I find the Boat Gang?"

The man pointed towards the top of the
huge pyramid. "Working up there today –

rather them than me!" he grunted.

Nephoris groaned. The sun raced on and this time it was winning.

As Nephoris reached the foot of the pyramid she saw her father and the Boat Gang stomping down with heavy feet and grim faces. "Just in time," she muttered. "He looks in a rotten temper. If he'd opened his lunch pack and found a rat... he might have eaten it in anger!"

Yenini glared at Nephoris. "What are you doing here? It's a dangerous place for a child. What is your mother thinking of? Wait until I get home."

"But I came to bring..." Nephoris began.

Then there was a rumble and the men of the Boat Gang turned and looked up at the pyramid.

At the top of the pyramid...

CHAPTER 4
Peril at the Pyramid

The Boat Gang had left their stone at the edge of the hole. The old wooden sledge grew hotter and drier in the midday sun. It creaked a little and then it cracked.

The stone sank into the sledge and turned it to splinters and dust. Finally the stone began to slip. It slipped steadily into the hole that was waiting for it. The stone landed with a "whumph" and settled.

It was a perfect fit. It would stay there until long after the Boat Gang had finished their work, long after Amenemhat was buried inside, long after the grave robbers had stolen his wealth. It would stay there until the end of time.

Yenini raced up the steep ramp. He was the fastest of the Lisht men – smooth and swift as his daughter. Nephoris ran behind him. She caught him up at the top of the pyramid. She could see clear across Lisht, over her village and over the mud-brown flowing Nile.

Her father's redness shrank to a spot on each cheek. The rest of his face and body was pale and sweating. "What's wrong?" Nephoris asked. "It fell where it was supposed to. It saved you the work!"

"We'll never get it out," her father whispered as the men of the Boat Gang panted and wheezed up to their side.

"Why would you want to get it out?" Nephoris asked, puzzled.

Yenini looked at her with haunted eyes. "Because little Antef is underneath that stone," he groaned. "Crushed."

"Like Oneney's beetles," Nephoris said.

"We've killed the king's man. Now the king will kill us," one of the workers moaned.

"It was an accident," Nephoris said.

"We all hated him," Yenini sighed. "No one will believe it was an accident."

"The king is coming this afternoon," a man said. "How do you think he will kill us?"

"Club us to death," someone suggested.

"Too quick and painless. Probably tie us to stakes in the desert and leave us to rot. Let the jackals eat us," another man argued.

They all began to wail and sob. "Throw us in a pit of poisoned snakes!" came one loud cry.

Suddenly a voice called out, louder than all the rest. "Stop it! Stop this pitiful noise!" Nephoris cried.

They stopped. They looked at the girl. "We're going to die-ie-ie!" an old man croaked.

"No you are not!" Nephoris said. "Get back to work. There is another stone waiting on the barge by the river. Get it on a sledge. Drag it up the pyramid. That's what you must be doing when the king arrives. Showing how hard you work for him – how much you worship him."

She waved a hand at the scene below. "Look! The Nile is flooding. Amenemhat has brought you life for another year. Let him see how much you love him. Get building!"

Yenini frowned. "He will want to see Antef driving us."

"And he will see Antef driving you," Nephoris promised.

"We can't pull him out from under the stone," a man argued.

"And if we did he'd be a bit... flat," Yenini argued.

"Just *do* it!" Nephoris said. "I'll have Antef with you by the time you have the next stone at the foot of the pyramid."

The men looked bewildered but

wandered back down the pyramid to obey her. Nephoris raced past them like a Nubian antelope and set off across the plain to Lisht.

King Amenemhat's boat drifted down the cool waters of the Nile and headed for Lisht...

CHAPTER 5
The Dead Driver

King Amenemhat was carried in a shaded chair. That's the only way for a god to travel. When he reached the pyramid he opened the curtain and looked out. His face was as calm as the carved lions in the temple, but inside he was excited.

He watched the Boat Gang heaving on the ropes and singing a

hymn. A hymn about their glorious King Amenemhat. His Majesty was pleased.

Walking alongside the Boat Gang was a little man with a perfumed wig and a plaited beard. Between the lines of the hymn the King could hear the little man shouting. It was not very pleasant.

"You are the biggest bunch of brainless

beetles on this pyramid and all you can do is sing. You can't move one little stone and you think it's something to sing about?" he shouted in his voice that was thin as a Nile reed.

He raised the whip and tried to crack it. The end of the whip lashed back and caught him on the end of his nose.

"Don't laugh, you rabble of rats! Ouch! Ouch! Ouch! If one man laughs I will have him taken to the top of the pyramid and thrown off! Now h-e-a-v-e!"

King Amenemhat said to a servant, "Send Antef to me."

The servant hurried off and brought the little work-driver back. Antef held a hand to his injured nose and kept his eyes on the sizzling sand. All King Amenemhat could see was the dark wig and the plaited beard.

"Is the work going well, Antef?" the king asked.

"Very, very well. We shall be finished by harvest time. That Boat Gang from Lisht are wonderful."

"You shout at them a lot!"

"Ah, but only because we all love you so much, we want to do better than our best for you." Antef said humbly.

"Better than your best. Is that the best you can do?"

"It's better," Antef muttered. "May I get back to work now, Your Majesty? They will be dropping that stone in place soon and I need to be there – we don't want any more accidents."

"Any more?" the king said. "Have there been any others?"

"No, Your Majesty," Antef said, a little confused. "Just the odd crushed beetle. Nothing to worry about."

"Beetles?"

"Crushed."

The king leaned forward and peered at the work-driver. "Are you all right, Antef?" Antef pulled out a large rag and covered his face with it.

"Sorry, Majesty," he sniffled. "It was my favourite beetle."

The king blew out his cheeks. "Antef. I think the sun has boiled your brain. Go home and rest until you feel better. Make one of the Boat Gang the new work-driver."

"Yenini is very good, Your Majesty."

"Very well, Yenini is the new work-driver," he said and leaned back. "Servants! Take me back to the palace."

The covered chair was carried away.

If the king had looked back he'd have seen Antef tear off the itching wig and the scratchy beard then run up the pyramid to where Yenini was waiting.

Antef ran with the stride of a gazelle and the padding fell out of his robes. He no longer looked like a fat little work-driver. He looked more like a girl called Nephoris hugging her father Yenini.

CHAPTER 6
Beard Wigs
and Earwigs

Nephoris walked home, arm in arm with her father, over the fields. She was carrying a purple robe, a perfumed wig and a beard wig. When they reached their village she handed them back to the artist Oneney and soon the fat statue of Antef was as good as new.

"I'm starving," Yenini said. "With all that bother at the pyramid I didn't even have time to eat my lunch."

"Your dinner is ready now," his wife said.

"No, it's a pity to waste good food," the man said. He pulled out his lunch packet and unwrapped it.

"Oh, Dad..." Nephoris began.

Too late. Yenini was staring at a fat, dead rat. He gave a roar that could be heard at the top of the pyramid. He threw the rat through the open doorway into the long grass with curses that would have frightened the demons of the underworld.

He was roaring so loudly he didn't hear the little cry of fear from the grass where the rat had landed.

But little Pere's sharp ears heard it. He pulled himself onto his stumpy legs and wandered out of the house. "Rats," he muttered.

The stars were burning in the purple sky and a thin moon glittered on the inky Nile. Pere carefully pulled the grass apart and saw the man lying there. A short, fat, bald man. The dead rat was resting on his bald head where it had landed. He was quivering and too terrified to move it.

"Rats," Pere said.

"Oh, little boy, hush. Don't give me away. Spare me and I'll see the king gives you a purse of gold. But don't tell the men of Lisht I am here."

"Little man," Pere said.

"They tried to kill me, you know. Left me in a hole and went to eat their lunch.

I was lucky. I caught one of the ropes on the sledge and pulled myself up. But I was a bit too heavy. I pulled the stone down. It fell just after I scrambled out. Oh, but I ran down the other side of the pyramid. They didn't see me. I bet they think they killed me!"

"Naughty man," Pere said. He picked up the dead rat and slapped Antef across the head with it. It fell to the ground.

"I've taken off my wig and beard so no one will know me," Antef babbled. "I've been hiding here all afternoon with the earwigs and spiders. When the moon sets I'll go down to the port and take the next boat out of Lisht. And I'll never come back. Never. They hate me."

Pere giggled.

"But I am so hungry," Antef groaned. "Can you give me something to eat, little boy? Please, please get me food – understand? Food. FOOD..."

Pere looked hard at the man with a face-crumpling frown. Then he smiled his one-toothed smile. He reached down to the ground and said, "Food!"

He picked up the rat and used his fat little fist to stuff it into Antef's mouth.

AFTERWORD

An old Greek writer called Herodotus went to Egypt thousands of years after the pyramids were build. The Egyptians told him they were built over ten years by 100,000 slaves.

Some school books still repeat the old Herodotus error, but the truth is...

- The pharaoh did not have 100,000 slaves in the whole of Egypt.
- Building each pyramid took around 25,000 men, and probably only five years.
- They were free men, not slaves, well fed with beef and ale – but paid only in food.
- There really were a lot of accidents on these dangerous building sites... although some may well have been deliberate!

YOU TRY

1. Build a statue

Can you build a small statue of Antef, like Oneney's? Use modelling clay for the body, and wool for the hair and plaited beard. Dress him in an Egyptian 'shendyt' – a kilt – made of paper. Look back at page 26, and do some extra research, to see how these things should look.

2. Pyramagic

A French shopkeeper called Antoine Bovis visited the Great Pyramid of Giza in the 1930s. He found the dead body of a stray cat that had wandered in – but Bovis noticed something amazing about the corpse of the cat. It had not turned rotten.

The cat seemed to be mummified, although it had never been through an embalming process. What explanation could he come up with? Had the pyramid itself preserved puss?

Bovis went back to France and experimented. He built model pyramids and left different types of food inside them. He found that the food kept inside a pyramid stayed fresh.

Is it true? Try it yourself. Research and draw a pyramid net on card, and then cut it out and build it. Perform the experiment by putting one piece of bread on a plate and another under your pyramid. Look at them a week later. Is the food under the pyramid fresher?